BREMNER
and the Party

Carrie Bolin and Jessica Firpi

Illustrated by John Graziano

RIPLEY
PUBLISHING

a Jim Pattison Company

My name is Bremner.
I'm a puffer fish.

I'm going to a party.

Gulp. Tonight.

What if no one
else shows up?

I'm sure everyone will already be there.

I bet they all know
each other.

IT'S A PARTY!

No one else will be nervous.

I hope I don't
puff up.

What if no one talks to me?

I really don't want to puff up.

Don't puff up. Don't puff up. Don't puff up.